SPACE PIRATES

Steve Barlow and Steve Skidmore

Illustrated by Santy Gutiérrez

EDGE

FRANKLIN WATTS

LONDON•SYDNEY

Franklin Watts
First published in Great Britain in 2019 by The Watts Publishing Group

Credits
Design Manager: Peter Scoulding
Cover Designer: Cathryn Gilbert
Illustrations: Santy Gutiérrez
HB ISBN 978 1 4451 5988 1
PB ISBN 978 1 4451 5989 8
Library ebook ISBN 978 1 4451 5990 4

Printed in China.

Franklin Watts
An imprint of
Hachette Children's Group
Part of The Watts Publishing Group
Carmelite House
50 Victoria Embankment
London EC4Y 0DZ

An Hachette UK Company
www.hachette.co.uk

www.franklinwatts.co.uk

THE BADDIES

Lord and Lady Evil	Dr Y

They want to rule the galaxy.

THE GOODIES

Boo Hoo   Jet   Tip

They want to stop them.

6

Master Boss told them about the
cargo ship. "We think it is full of gold.
We want you to steal it!"

"Great!" said Jet.

"We are going to be Space Pirates!"
said Tip. "Oo-ar!"

Jet shook her head. "Not funny."

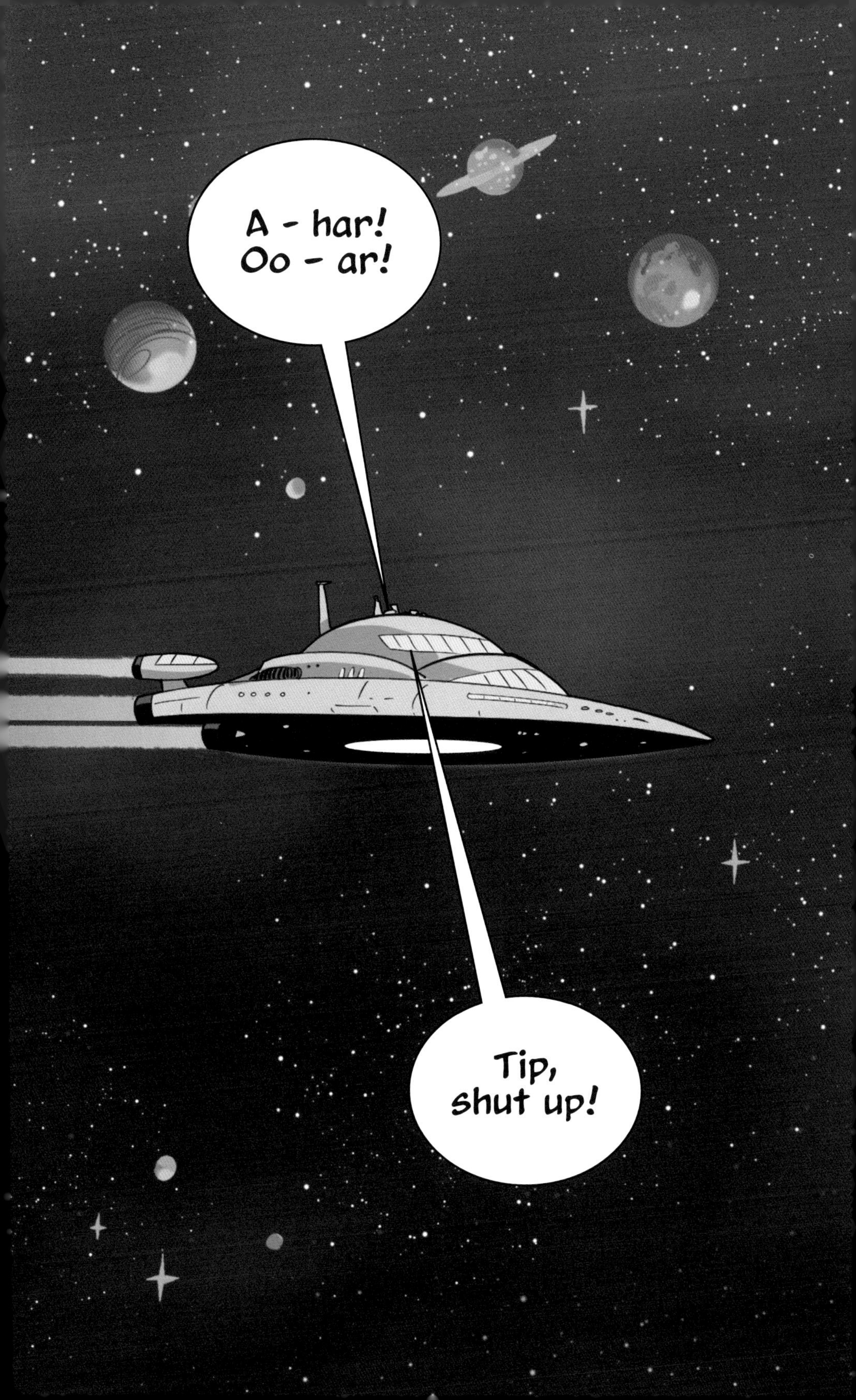
A - har! Oo - ar!
Tip, shut up!

16

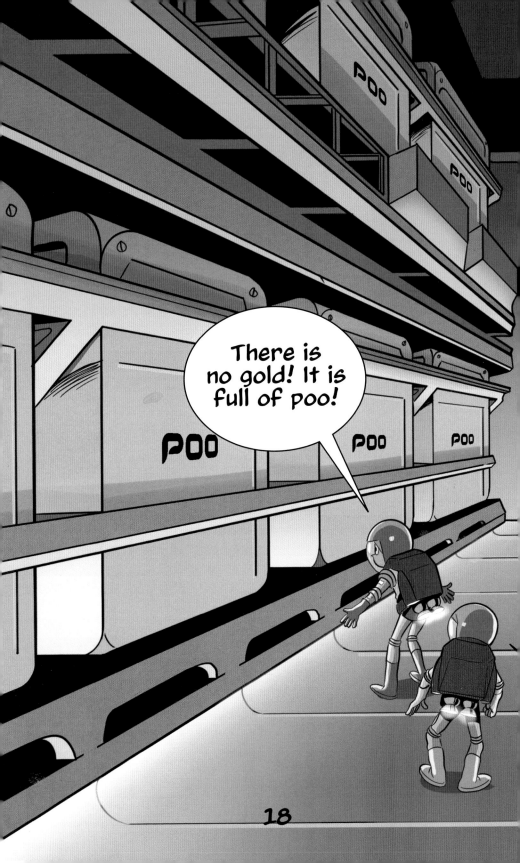

19

Dr Y spoke up. "I have a new report."

"What is it?" said Lady Evil.

"Tip and Jet are on the cargo ship."

On the cargo ship.
The Baddies are coming!
RADAR
Let's leave them a present!

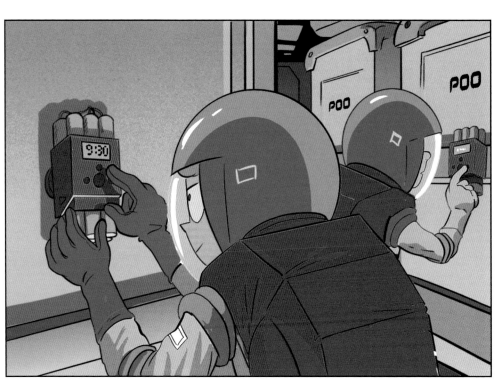

23

Tip and Jet set the explosive charges.

They went back to Shawn the Ship.

Minutes later, the Baddies arrived.

They headed onto the cargo ship.

25

27

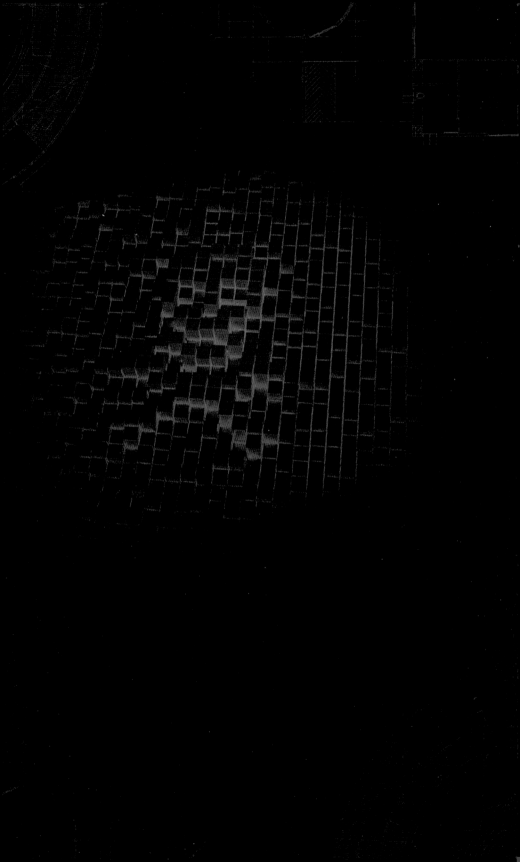